FLIPPY FROG KEEPS FIT

BY JUNE WOODMAN

ILLUSTRATED BY PAMELA STOREY

GONDOLA

It is a very hot day.
The sun is out and the
flowers are out. Flippy Frog
is out too. He likes to swim
in the pond on very hot days.
He jumps into the pond . . .
PLOP!
He swims off very fast.
Then Flippy begins to huff
and Flippy begins to puff.
"I am not fit," he says.

He swims to the other side of the pond and hops out . . . PLOP!

Then he hops off to look for Dilly Duck. He hops along very fast. But soon he begins to huff and puff.

He sits down on the grass to have a rest. The sun is hot and Flippy Frog is hot too. "I am not fit," he says.

Here comes Dilly Duck.
She runs after her three
little ducklings. She cannot
catch them. Dilly begins to
huff and puff.
"You are not fit, Dilly," says
Flippy Frog. "Come with me."
"Where are you going?" says
Dilly Duck.
"To the Keep Fit Class,"
says Flippy Frog.

Here comes Hoppy Rabbit.
His car will not go. Hoppy
begins to push it. But the
sun is hot and he huffs and
he puffs.
Bossy Bear comes by on his
roller-skates. He begins to
huff and puff too.
"You are NOT FIT!" says
Flippy Frog. "Come with us
to the Keep Fit Class."

"Look at Paddy Dog on his scooter," say the three little ducklings.
Paddy goes very fast, but he huffs and puffs.
Cuddly Cat runs after a big butterfly. She huffs and she puffs, but she cannot catch it.
"Come with us to the Keep Fit Class," says Flippy Frog.
Off they go down the lane.

They come to a big barn
and they all go inside.
"Here we are!" says Flippy.
"Now do what I do."
He gets a big ball and he
throws it up into a net.
The ball comes down on to
Flippy Frog's head . . .
BUMP!
"That is no good," says Bossy.

Flippy gets a long rope.
"Do what I do, Cuddly Cat,"
he says. "Then you will get
fit too."
But the rope is too long
and Flippy falls over it.
Down goes poor Flippy Frog . . .
BUMP!
"That is no good," says
Cuddly Cat.

Flippy runs up to a big bag.
He begins to hit it.
"Do what I do," he says to
the three little ducklings.
Flippy hits the bag, but the
bag comes back and hits him.
Down goes poor Flippy Frog . . .
BUMP!
"That is no good," says
Bossy Bear.

Paddy Dog runs by.
"Look!" he says. "I can
throw the ball and catch it."
"Look at Paddy!" say the
ducklings. "He can catch the
big ball. That is very good.
Paddy Dog is very fit."
But Flippy Frog is cross.

Cuddly Cat runs by.
"Look at me!" she says.
"I can skip, but I do not
fall down."
She can skip very fast.
"Look at Cuddly!" say the
ducklings. "That is very
good."
Cuddly runs and skips with
the rope, but she does not
fall. Flippy does not look.
Flippy Frog is very cross.

Bossy and Hoppy go up to the big bag. They begin to hit it. They are very good.

"Look at Bossy and Hoppy!" say the three little ducklings.

Flippy does not look.

Flippy Frog is VERY cross.

"He IS funny," say the three little ducklings.

"He is SILLY!" says Dilly.

"I shall keep fit in my own way. Come with me."

Dilly Duck and her ducklings go back to the duck pond. Cuddly Cat and Bossy Bear go with them. Paddy Dog and Hoppy Rabbit run after them. Last of all comes poor Flippy Frog. He does not look very fit. He hops after them all the way back to the duck pond. He huffs and he puffs.

Dilly Duck is in the pond.
She swims up and down.
She does not huff and she
does not puff.
The three little ducklings
jump into the pond after her.
PLOP! PLOP! PLOP!
"This is the best way for
ducks to keep fit," says
Dilly Duck.
"It is the best way for
frogs too!" says Flippy.
PLOP!

Say these words again

flowers

jumps

own

along

catch

where

push

butterfly

barn

throws

shall

good

rope

what

ZOO BABIES

Nanuck the Polar Bear

Story by **Georgeanne Irvine**
Photographs by **Ron Garrison**

of the **Zoological Society of San Diego**

School & Library Edition
CHILDRENS PRESS, CHICAGO

Library of Congress Cataloging in Publication Data

Irvine, Georgeanne.
  Nanuck the polar bear.

  (Zoo babies)
  Includes index.
  Summary: A polar bear baby in the zoo hates
the idea of swimming, and nothing his mother
does can tempt him into the water.
  1. Polar bear—Juvenile literature.
2. Animals, Infancy of—Juvenile literature.
3. Zoo animals—Juvenile literature.   [1. Polar
bear. 2. Animals—Infancy. 3. Zoo animals]
I. Garrison, Ron, ill. II. Title. III. Series.
QL737.C27I78 1982   599.74′446   82-9463
ISBN 0-516-09302-9   AACR2

ZOO BABIES

Nanuck the Polar Bear

Everybody knows that all polar
bears love to swim—all except me.
I'm Nanuck, a polar bear!

I'd better explain that I do know I'm
supposed to be a great swimmer.
When I was growing up in the Zoo
though, I was afraid of the water for a
long time, and I did not love to swim!

I didn't even get near water until I was three months old. The bear keeper kept my mother, Bonnie, and me by ourselves for my first three months. Because I was quite tiny, it was important to keep us away from noise and other things that might bother us.

My first time out in the big polar
bear exhibit was very interesting.
Mother told me that the walls were
painted white to look like the snowy
Arctic where my polar bear relatives
live. My fur looked yellow next to the
white walls of the exhibit.

I couldn't wait to go exploring.

There was one thing Mother warned me about—the big pool of water right in the middle of our bear home. Mother said she'd teach me all about water and swimming when I was a little older.

I didn't listen. Her warning made
me more curious than ever to explore
the big pool. I crept over to the edge
of the pool and stretched out my paw
to touch the water. I stretched a bit
too far! Down I went—right into the
pool with a great big SPLASH!

HELP! I was wet, cold, and frightened! Mother came to the rescue and pulled me out by the scruff of my neck.

That did it! No more water or swimming for me—EVER!

I stayed close to Mother after that. Wherever she went, I went—except when she went swimming, of course.

Days and then weeks went by. I grew older and bigger. Mother decided that it was time for me to start swimming.

She did everything she could to get me to dive into the water. Mother would splash me with water, and I'd go hide.

She'd chase me around the pool and nudge me toward the water, but I'd slip away. She dove into the pool to make swimming look like fun, but it didn't change my mind.

Mother said our polar bear bodies
are made for swimming. She said our
skin is oily which helps protect it from
the water. We have a thick layer of fat
to help us float. Our toes even have
webbing between them, so our feet
push us like the swim fins that people
wear.

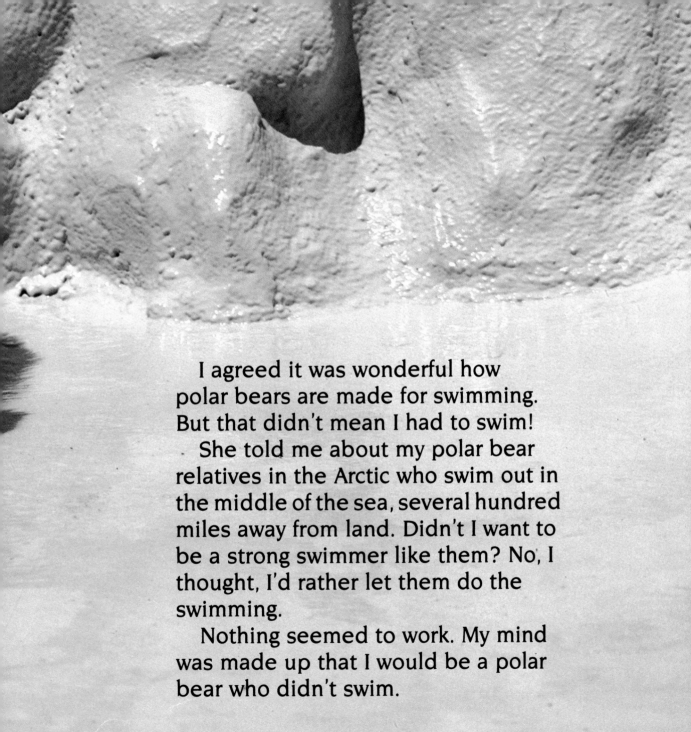

I agreed it was wonderful how polar bears are made for swimming. But that didn't mean I had to swim!

She told me about my polar bear relatives in the Arctic who swim out in the middle of the sea, several hundred miles away from land. Didn't I want to be a strong swimmer like them? No, I thought, I'd rather let them do the swimming.

Nothing seemed to work. My mind was made up that I would be a polar bear who didn't swim.

One day the bear keeper came to
the front of our enclosure with a fish
in his hand. I had become so big that
I was eating fish like Mother does. I
would do anything for a fish.

The bear keeper tossed a fish to me. SPLASH! It landed right in the middle of the pool! Oh, how I wanted that fish!

Slowly I crept over to the edge of the pool. I could already taste the fish in my mouth. SPLASH! I was in the pool, but I had my fish.

Being in the water didn't seem that bad! As a matter of fact, it was rather nice.

Since that day, Mother can seldom get me out of the water. I am now a polar bear who loves to swim!

Facts About Polar Bears

Where found: the ice and snow, where her baby or babies are born.

Adult polar bears: Polar bears are longer and thinner than other kinds of bears. The adult is about nine or ten feet in length and weighs about 1,000 pounds or more.

Fur: A very thick coat of fur helps keep polar bears warm in the cold Arctic air and water. The fur is not actually pure white. It has a creamy or yellowy shade to it. It is still light enough to make the bears difficult to see with the ice and snow all around it. And this makes it easy for polar bears to sneak up on the animals it kills for food.

Feet: The soles of their feet are thick and hairy. This helps the bears to walk on the ice and snow without slipping and sliding around. It also keeps their feet warm.

Food: Polar bears eat fish, seals, and other Arctic animals.

Swimming: Polar bears are the best swimmers of all bears, partly because of their Polar bears live only in the Arctic. That is the cold, snowy land and ice around the North Pole. (No polar bears live in the Antarctic, the land around the South Pole.)

Family: Polar bears are members of the bear family, they are the only bears that are white in color.

Baby polar bears: Babies weigh about one pound each at birth. Only one or two cubs, as they are called, are born at a time.

INDEX